P9-APK-709

Minnesota Timberwolves

John Nichols

CREATIVE C EDUCATION

Published by Creative Education
123 South Broad Street, Mankato, Minnesota 56001
Creative Education is an imprint of The Creative Company

Designed by Rita Marshall

Photos by: Allsport Photography, Associated Press/Wide World Photos,
Focus on Sports, NBA Photos, UPI/Corbis-Bettmann, and SportsChrome.

Photo page 1: Stephon Marbury
Photo title page: Tom Gugliotta

Library of Congress Cataloging-in-Publication Data

Nichols, John, 1966–
Minnesota Timberwolves / John Nichols.
p. cm.—(NBA today)
Summary: Describes the background and history of the Minnesota
Timberwolves pro basketball team.
ISBN 0-88682-881-3

1. Minnesota Timberwolves (Basketball team)—History—Juvenile literature.
[1. Minnesota Timberwolves (Basketball team)—History. 2. Basketball—
History.]
I. Title. II. Series: NBA today (Mankato, Minn.)

GV885.52.M565N53 1997   96-51057
796.323'64'09776579—dc21

Minnesota, the state known as the land of 10,000 lakes, is also home to nearly three million people who live in and around Minneapolis and St. Paul. Minnesota's Twin Cities, located on the eastern border of the state, share many attractions, including the Mississippi River, which runs through both cities and provides industry and entertainment for residents and visitors alike. The people of the area are known for being hearty folk who enjoy the variety of seasons found in their northern climate.

The Twin Cities are also home to several professional sports franchises, including the Minnesota Vikings of the Na-

The state-of-the-art Target Center.

Former Lakers star George Mikan led a panel to help bring basketball back to Minnesota.

tional Football League and the Minnesota Twins of Major League Baseball. Minnesota's first pro team, however, played basketball. The National Basketball Association's (NBA) Minneapolis Lakers began play in the late 1940s, and were the dominant team in the league during the early 1950s. Led by Hall of Fame center George Mikan, the Minneapolis Lakers won an incredible five league championships between 1949 and 1954. The Lakers stayed in Minneapolis until the end of the 1960 season, when mismanagement and dwindling attendance forced the team to move to Los Angeles. Though the Lakers were gone, Minnesotans never gave up on pro basketball. When the NBA began considering expansion in the mid-1980s, Minnesota was proud to present itself as an attractive market. When it was announced in 1987 that there would be a new team in Minneapolis called the Timberwolves, there was much excitement in the Twin Cities and around the state.

The team played its first season in the Hubert H. Humphrey Metrodome, home of the Vikings and Twins but in 1990 a new arena was built just for the Wolves. The state-of-the-art 19,000-seat Target Center is the only arena in the United States with a movable floor that has ice-making capabilities. Fans who had seen such past greats as Mikan and Elgin Baylor make basketball history now fill the Target Center to embrace a new crop of heroes. Today's stars—Kevin Garnett, Tom Gugliotta, and Stephon Marbury—hope to write a new championship history for Minnesota. With native son and former Boston Celtics great Kevin McHale in control of the front office, it shouldn't be long before Minnesota is cheering for a new winner.

Kevin Garnett, a young star on the rise.

1 9 8 8

Bill Musselman, twice voted CBA Coach of the Year, was named the Wolves' first head coach.

After being awarded the franchise, Timberwolves owners Harvey Ratner and Marv Wolfenson began their search for the team's first coach. They knew it was important to find a coach who could squeeze the most out of each man, because a first-year team wouldn't have much talent. The Timberwolves needed a motivator, a teacher, and—most of all—a person who was mentally tough. With those qualifications in mind, the team chose Bill Musselman to be their first head coach.

Musselman was a familiar face to Twin Cities basketball fans. As a college coach, he had led the University of Minnesota to a Big Ten Conference championship in 1971–72. He also had previous pro coaching experience in the NBA with the Cleveland Cavaliers. But Musselman's most impressive work was done in the Continental Basketball Association (CBA), a lower-level professional league. His CBA teams won four straight league championships from 1985 through 1988, and because of this success, Musselman had earned another opportunity in the NBA. "It's great to be here," said Musselman. "Now let's build a winner."

With their coach selected, attention turned towards finding players. The first Timberwolves team would be built through the annual college draft and a special NBA expansion draft. The expansion draft allowed the two new teams—the Timberwolves and the Orlando Magic—to select from a pool of players left unprotected by teams already in the league. Musselman and team president Bob Stein knew that out of the available players in the expansion pool, there would be few, if any, with the ability to be starters in the NBA. The talent was thin, so careful choices had to be made.

CORBIN AND RICHARDSON: FIRST WOLVES

1 9 8 9

Tod Murphy had a three-point field goal percentage of .372 to lead the first-year Wolves.

When the Timberwolves were able to land 6-foot-6 forward Tyrone Corbin from the Phoenix Suns in the expansion draft, Musselman breathed a sigh of relief. "Ty is a first-rate rebounder. He can score and he plays defense with pride," said an excited Musselman. "We were shocked to see him available." Corbin had been a standout in college with the DePaul Blue Demons, but had not been able to get much playing time on a very good Suns team.

"I was so happy to come to Minnesota and finally get a chance," said a smiling Corbin. "I knew I could play, and when I got my shot I wasn't going to let it get away." Corbin brought veteran backbone to a team that was out-gunned in the talent department nearly every time out. If the Wolves needed rebounding, Corbin did it. If the team needed scoring, Corbin delivered it. If the team needed defense, Corbin could provide it. Corbin's never-say-die attitude sparked his team to believe it could do the impossible.

"Some nights you'd look out and see Ty guarding a big guy like Karl Malone, who's got him by three inches and 30 pounds, and he'd be doing a good job," remembered teammate Tony Campbell. "He made me a believer that effort was everything in this game."

The Wolves gave Corbin some help when they selected UCLA point guard Jerome "Pooh" Richardson with the 10th pick in the college draft. Many NBA talent scouts believed

The hustling Ty Corbin.

A master ball handler, Pooh Richardson.

In a game against the Clippers, Randy Breuer pulled down 13 rebounds to lead the team.

that the Wolves had rated Richardson too highly, considering him no better than a second-round pick. But the coach saw more. "Pooh plays and acts like a guy much more experienced than he is," said Musselman. "He's a true point guard who is more concerned about distributing the ball to the right man and not so worried about his own offense."

Despite his high opinion of Richardson, Musselman did not start the young guard to begin the season. Musselman believed starting spots had to be earned and not given to rookies. Although Musselman started Richardson midway through the season, a seed of disagreement between the coach and his rookie had been planted that would continue to grow during Musselman's time in Minnesota.

"Coach and I have a weird relationship," observed Richardson. "We both want to win so bad, but we have different philosophies on how to do it."

Richardson wanted to push the ball up the floor and take advantage of his open-court skills. Musselman believed the only way the Wolves could be competitive was to play a half-court game, relying on tough defense to win. Using Musselman's conservative style, the Wolves posted a record of 26–56 their first season (1989–90). Then, when Musselman gradually opened up the offense and gave more time to the team's younger players, the Wolves improved to 29–53 in their second year (1990–91). Richardson blossomed as a floor leader, and the Wolves received strong contributions from Campbell and Corbin. But despite the improved record, the clash of philosophies between Musselman and his players continued to escalate. After much public debate, the Wolves' front office intervened on the side of the players, firing Musselman in the off-season.

"I don't think this team can get any better until we find out where the young guys on this team are going to take us," explained team president Dick Stein at Musselman's firing. Jimmy Rodgers, former head coach of the Boston Celtics, was named Musselman's successor, and he quickly cast aside all doubts about what style of basketball the Wolves would play. "We're going to run," pronounced a steadfast Rodgers.

Center Luc Longley became the first native Australian to play in an NBA game (at Dallas).

But Rodgers's attempts to turn the team over to the younger players didn't translate into victories. In fact, with Rodgers at the helm, the club took a big step backward, finishing the season with a 15–67 mark. Minnesota was also feeling the impact of two years of bad luck in the NBA draft lottery. Despite poor records during their first two seasons, the Wolves never picked high enough to land a top player. The choices of sturdy centers Felton Spencer and Luc Longley in successive years did little to improve the Wolves' sluggish offense. To make matters worse, the team traded stalwart forward Ty Corbin to the Utah Jazz for aging big man Thurl Bailey in a misguided attempt to give the Wolves some inside strength. All these factors contributed to what was just the beginning of a long nightmare for the Wolves.

TRADER JACK ADDS LAETTNER TO ATTACK

After the disastrous 1991–92 season, the Timberwolves knew they needed a proven winner to manage the

Tony Campbell had the Wolves' highest scoring average (16.8) for the third season in a row.

team. Jack McCloskey, the man who had built the Detroit Pistons into two-time NBA champions, was hired to be the Wolves' general manager. McCloskey, known as Trader Jack due to his reputation for making trades, didn't wait long to make changes. In the draft, the Wolves used their highest pick ever to take Duke University center Christian Laettner third overall. The 6-foot-11 Laettner had built up quite a resume while in college. He led Duke to two national championships, and was named college basketball's Player of the Year in 1992. Laettner was also the only college player named to the 1992 U.S. Olympic Dream Team. The opportunity to play and win a gold medal with NBA legends Larry Bird and Michael Jordan gave Laettner an idea of what it took to excel in the NBA.

"Playing on the Dream Team taught me that stars are made not born," said Laettner. "The guys like Michael, Larry, and Patrick Ewing worked hard every day. They don't ever let up. That's the secret."

Laettner's combination of size and quickness made him a perfect fit as an NBA power forward. The Timberwolves liked his game, but what they were most impressed by was his winning attitude. The team hoped that Laettner's fiery competitiveness would inject new life into the franchise. But other NBA experts feared a different drama might unfold. Laettner's Dream Team coach, Chuck Daly, expressed his worries after the Olympics. "Laettner gives Minnesota a talent they can build around," observed Daly. "He's a tough kid, but I don't know if he'll be able to handle the losing he's going to experience right away."

After adding Laettner, McCloskey traded Pooh Richardson

A Wolves first-round draft pick, Christian Laettner.

and Sam Mitchell to the Indiana Pacers for "Rifleman" Chuck Person, and point guard Micheal Williams. The Wolves started the season with six new faces in the lineup and got off to a decent 4–7 start, but then the cold winds of December brought a month of losing that saw the team win only one game out of 13.

Daly's predictions were realized: Laettner, unable to carry the team by himself, experienced more losses in three weeks with the Timberwolves then he had in four years at Duke. Frustrated by the losing streak, Laettner and Person began to criticize the front office and each other. Lacking any chem-

1 9 9 3

Chuck Person went 6-for-6 from three-point range in a game vs. Miami.

Tom Gugliotta, a promise for the future.

istry, the team self-destructed. On January 11, former Wolves' player Sydney Lowe was named as interim coach, replacing Rodgers. Lowe had retired as a player after 1990, and had worked as a Timberwolves television broadcaster until taking an assistant coaching position with the team in 1991. Lowe, the youngest head coach in the NBA at 33, temporarily smoothed over tensions on the team. But the Wolves still struggled to a 19–63 record. In March, Lowe was elevated from interim coach to head coach.

Guard Isaiah "J.R." Rider was named to the NBA's All-Rookie first team.

WOLVES LAND ROUGH RIDER

In an effort to give the team some scoring punch at guard, the Timberwolves chose University of Nevada-Las Vegas guard Isaiah "J.R." Rider with the fifth pick. The 6-foot-5 Rider brought explosiveness to the team in more ways than one. He was fast, strong, and could practically jump out of the gym. But throughout his college career he had been criticized for having a lack of discipline and for not playing hard all the time. "Isaiah is a young guy," said Lowe about his rookie. "And young guys can drive you crazy. But we have to be patient and let him grow."

In Isaiah Rider, the Timberwolves had a brilliant athletic talent, but also acquired another strong personality on a team that already featured the vocal Laettner and Person. Rider had several run-ins with the law during his career in Minnesota, and for every off-court problem he had, there were twice as many infractions of team rules. His habit of missing team planes and meetings got Rider into more trouble than his enormous talent could ever get him out of. The

The competitive Christian Laettner (pages 18–19).

Wolves had yet another poor season, finishing with a record of 20–62. But Rider, despite his problems, did provide some great highlights for the fans: he won the Gatorade Slam-Dunk Championship at the All-Star Weekend in Minneapolis, finishing his performance with a between-the-legs, one-handed dunk he called the "East Bay Funk."

1 9 9 5

In a 104-92 win over Detroit, Donyell Marshall shared high points honors (25) with Christian Laettner.

THE "BAD DREAM" CONTINUES

Despite great attendance, the Timberwolves were almost sold to an ownership group that wanted to move the team to New Orleans for 1994–95. Fortunately for the supportive Minnesota fans, the NBA voted down the sale, and Minnesota businessman Glen Taylor bought the Timberwolves, promising to keep them in the state. As a former state legislator and the owner of many successful Minnesota businesses, Taylor knew that the purchase of a sports team could be a financial risk—but he also had faith in the young Timberwolves' potential for success.

The new ownership replaced Sydney Lowe at head coach with Bill Blair and selected University of Connecticut forward Donyell Marshall in the draft that spring. Among all of these changes taking place, Minnesota fans were hoping for better days.

But things still weren't going right for the Wolves. They had a roster loaded with high draft picks, but their play wasn't getting any better. "I don't know. I just don't know," said Laettner. "Sometimes it just seems like a bad dream and that we'll wake up from it." With the team already buried in the standings by mid-season, the Wolves took their first step toward recovery. They decided to trade disappointing Donyell Marshall, and didn't expect to get much in return. Marshall had been a giant flop, and trading him was an effort to cut their losses. So when the Golden State Warriors offered the highly productive Tom Gugliotta, Minnesota could hardly believe their good fortune.

"I point to getting 'Googs' as a turning point for us as a franchise," said Doug West, who had been with the Timberwolves since day one. "He brought us a lot of talent, hard work, and zero bad attitude."

Former Boston Celtics great Kevin McHale added seven new players to the Wolves' opening day lineup.

The 6-foot-10, 240-pound Gugliotta had come out of North Carolina State University as a first-round draft pick of the Washington Bullets in 1992. After playing two rock-solid seasons for the Bullets, Gugliotta was traded to Golden State as part of a deal to bring Chris Webber to the Bullets. After posting solid numbers in limited time with the Warriors, he was dealt again to Minnesota. "I was happy to come to Minnesota," said Gugliotta, "because I knew they wanted me here and I finally felt at home after all the trades."

Gugliotta provided instant help for the Timberwolves. He filled up the stat sheet, averaging 14.4 points, 7.2 rebounds, and 4.5 assists per game the rest of the year. His versatility became his trademark, as Gugliotta was among the team leaders in all categories, whether it was rebounding, assists, or three-point shooting. With the addition of Gugliotta, the Wolves showed signs of life in the season's second half, but still finished 1994–95 with a dismal 21–61 record. The Timberwolves had set an NBA record, though it wasn't one they were proud of. They became the first team ever to lose 60 games a year for four straight years.

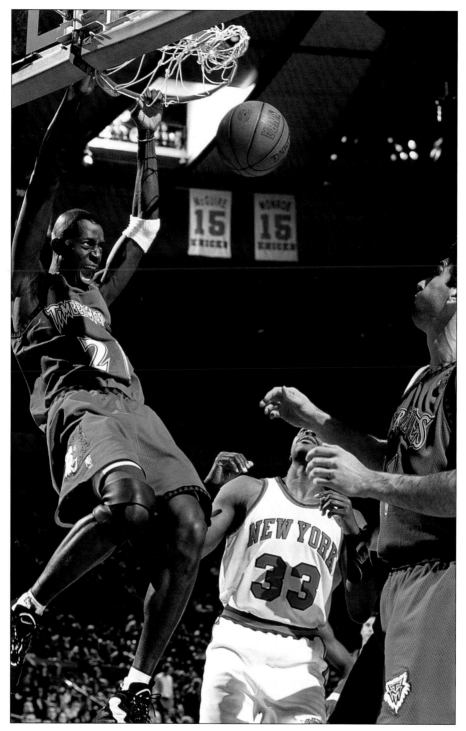

The agile Kevin Garnett.

At season's end, former Boston Celtics star and native Minnesotan Kevin McHale took over as the Timberwolves vice president of basketball operations, replacing retiring general manager Jack McCloskey. McHale promised fans when he took the job that he would make bold moves to shake the team out of its losing rut. He didn't take long to make good on that promise.

The only original Timberwolves player still on the team, Doug West played in a record 503 games.

GARNETT BECOMES A TEEN WOLF

With the fifth pick in the 1995 draft, Minnesota took the young 6-foot-11 forward, Kevin Garnett. Many NBA experts thought the team had made another draft mistake. It wasn't that the critics thought Garnett didn't have ability. It was widely agreed upon that he had the talent to become a superstar in the NBA . . . someday. But at age 19? It seemed so. When he was drafted, Garnett became only the fourth player to go straight from high school to the NBA, joining the ranks of Moses Malone, Bill Willoughby, and Shawn Kemp. Garnett was an extraordinary talent, combining the agility and speed of a quick guard with the leaping ability and soft touch that made him deadly around the basket.

"Don't let that skinny body fool you," joked Los Angeles Lakers great Kareem Abdul-Jabbar. "Kevin's an NBA player now. I just worry about how he'll handle the other stuff." By the "other stuff," Abdul-Jabbar meant money, media demands, and the constant pressure to perform that goes along with being a professional athlete. The Timberwolves were so concerned about Garnett's well being that they moved his mother up from Chicago to live with him, providing a stable

23

Terry Porter led the Timberwolves in assists with 452 for the season.

home life during his first year in the league. Still, many feared that the pressures and temptations of the NBA would be too much for a young man barely out of high school.

"Kevin has enormous talent and potential," said McHale. "He can be a very special player in this league, but we have to take every right step in developing him." Every right step meant that McHale needed to instill a positive attitude in his team. Some of the veterans had grown frustrated with the years of losing, and were disappointed that the team had drafted a player who would need time to develop. McHale decided that more changes needed to be made.

In December, he replaced head coach Bill Blair with Phil "Flip" Saunders, who had been McHale's teammate at the University of Minnesota in the 1970s. After his college career, Saunders had gone on to coach in the CBA, where he eventually won two championships. Saunders got the job based on his reputation as a coach who could turn bad teams into winners in a short period of time. Also, he and McHale shared a common vision of what needed to be done to make the Wolves competitive. Along with the coaching change, McHale also made a big trade. Christian Laettner and Sean Rooks were shipped to the Atlanta Hawks for Andrew Lang and Spud Webb. It seemed that Laettner had become expendable because of the remarkable development of Garnett. All the concerns over Garnett's age faded with each eye-opening blocked shot and slam dunk he made. "The Kid," as his teammates called him, was going to be the real deal, real soon. Lifted up by the emergence of their young star, the Wolves had their best season since 1991, finishing at 25–56.

One thing Timberwolves' fans could always count on, from the very first tip-off in team history, was steady swingman Doug West. West was taken by Minnesota in the second round of the 1989 draft from Villanova University, and had been there ever since. "When I think about Doug being the only original guy still here, I think it's a testament to his strong will," said Timberwolves coach Flip Saunders. "He's never let any of the team's problems or the years of losing get him down."

Indeed, West has been a pillar of strength for the Timberwolves. Year in and year out, West gave the Wolves solid if not spectacular play at both shooting guard and small forward. West's quick first step made him an offensive threat, but his forte was defense. His experience in college basketball's physical Big East conference taught him that shutting down the opponent would be his ticket to the show.

"I take more pride in my defense than anything," said West. "I think that's a big reason I'm still here. A lot of guys can score but not many want to put in the work to play good 'D.'" West had played for five different Timberwolves coaches, two different ownership groups, and prior to 1996–97 had never played on a team that had won more than 30 games. But he never gave up. "I just want to be a part of this thing when we get it turned around," said West, almost as though he were predicting the future.

1 9 9 7

By his second stretch with the team, Sam Mitchell had played more than 300 games with the Wolves.

Sam Mitchell, powerful under the boards (pages 26–27).

1 9 9 7

Coach Phil (Flip) Saunders guided the Timberwolves to their first playoff appearance in club history.

Encouraged by the impact of Kevin Garnett, the Timberwolves acquired another youthful phenom in 1996, when they traded the rights to their first-round pick (Ray Allen of Connecticut) and a future first-round pick to the Milwaukee Bucks for the rights to Georgia Tech guard Stephon Marbury. Marbury had played only one season at Georgia Tech before deciding to turn pro, making him the second consecutive teenager drafted by the Wolves.

A native of New York City, Marbury had already become a playground legend by the time he was 13 years old. As a senior at Abraham Lincoln High School, he was named the National High School Player of the Year by *Parade* Magazine. In one season at Georgia Tech, the upstart freshman earned First Team Atlantic Coast Conference honors and was a third team All-American. "Stephon can do it all," said Garnett about his new teammate. "I don't think it'll be long before we make a pretty scary combination."

The 19-year-old Marbury's ability to handle the ball and create offensive chances for his teammates and himself gave the Wolves another weapon in their improving arsenal. The Wolves also traded troubled Isaiah Rider to the Portland Trail Blazers for guard James Robinson, forward Bill Curley, and future considerations. Rider's continuing snags with the police had soured the Wolves on his great talent. His off-court problems and uneven play had become a distraction and a worry that the Wolves just couldn't afford. McHale made the tough decision to trade Rider in order to give his young players the most positive atmosphere in which to develop

Rookie standout Stephon Marbury.

One of the Wolves' brightest stars, Tom Gugliotta.

Dean Garrett, an aggressive shot blocker. 31

1 9 9 7

Stephon Marbury, second in Rookie of the Year voting, was named to the All-Rookie team.

for 1996–97. He had learned from his days with the champion Celtics that maintaining good chemistry between players, coaches, and fans was sometimes more important than focusing on one player's ability.

"J.R. has great talent, but we need a commitment to winning," said McHale. "We think that with the people we have right now we can start making good on that commitment."

And make good they did. With a lean past behind them, the 1996–97 Timberwolves finally appeared to be on track for greatness. For the first time in franchise history, the team made it to the NBA playoffs. Although eliminated in the first round by the Houston Rockets, the Wolves made their opponent work hard for their wins. With a nucleus that includes Garnett, Marbury, and Gugliotta, it should be just a matter of time and seasoning before the Wolves write another chapter of championship basketball history in Minnesota.